Slinky Malinki,
Early Bird

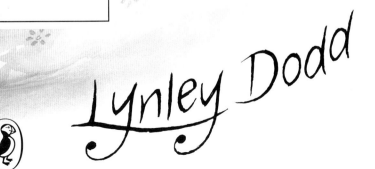

Lynley Dodd

PUFFIN

Early one morning
when all were asleep,
Slinky Malinki
decided to creep
out of his bed
in the shadowy gloom,
and off on the prowl
by the light
of the moon.

Past the piano
and wickerwork chairs,
he silently padded
to climb up the stairs.

'WRRROW?'
he said,
as he slipped through each door
to wake up the family,
one, two, three, four.

He purred in their ears

and he pounced on their toes,

he bristled his whiskers
and tickled each nose.

'PESKY OLD SLINKY!'
 the family moaned,
'You woke us TOO EARLY!'
 they grumbled and groaned.
'PLEASE
 leave us in peace
 for an hour or two!'
 But
 Slinky Malinki knew
 just
 what
 to
 do.

He bounced like a ball

and he played hide and seek,

he sang yowly songs
and he smooched every cheek.

He tipped over lamps
and he sat on their heads,

until he had pestered them
out of their beds.

They mumbled and moaned
as they stomped down the stairs,
they grumbled and groaned
as they flopped into chairs,
'We wanted some PEACE
for an hour or two!'
But
Slinky Malinki knew
just
what
to
do.

He patiently waited
then,
turning instead,

Slinky Malinki went
straight
back
to
bed.

PUFFIN BOOKS
Published by the Penguin Group
Penguin Group (NZ), 67 Apollo Drive, Rosedale,
Auckland 0632, New Zealand (a division of Pearson New Zealand Ltd)
Penguin Group (USA) Inc., 375 Hudson Street, New York, New York 10014, USA
Penguin Group (Canada), 90 Eglinton Avenue East, Suite 700, Toronto,
Ontario, M4P 2Y3, Canada (a division of Pearson Penguin Canada Inc.)
Penguin Books Ltd, 80 Strand, London, WC2R 0RL, England
Penguin Ireland, 25 St Stephen's Green, Dublin 2, Ireland (a division of Penguin Books Ltd)
Penguin Group (Australia), 250 Camberwell Road, Camberwell, Victoria 3124, Australia (a division of Pearson Australia Group Pty Ltd)
Penguin Books India Pvt Ltd, 11, Community Centre, Panchsheel Park, New Delhi – 110 017, India
Penguin Books (South Africa) (Pty) Ltd, 24 Sturdee Avenue, Rosebank, Johannesburg 2196, South Africa

Penguin Books Ltd, Registered Offices: 80 Strand, London, WC2R 0RL, England

Published by Puffin Books, 2012
1 3 5 7 9 10 8 6 4 2

Copyright © Lynley Dodd, 2012

Designed and typeset by Cochran & Norman, Wellington, New Zealand
Prepress by Image Centre Ltd
Printed in China by South China Printing Company

A catalogue record for this book is available from the National Library of New Zealand.

www.penguin.co.nz

Also available: